Watch Out for Strangers

Acknowledgments
Executive Editor: Diane Sharpe
Supervising Editor: Stephanie Muller
Design Manager: Sharon Golden
Page Design: Ian Winton
Photography: Chris Fairclough: cover (top right); Image Bank: cover (left), page 14; Alex Ramsay: pages 9, 11, 17, 21, 23, 24.

ISBN 0-8114-3724-8

Copyright © 1995 Steck-Vaughn Company

All rights reserved. No part of the material protected by this copyright may be reproduced or utilized in any form or by any means, electronic or mechanical, including photocopying, recording, or by any information storage and retrieval system, without permission in writing from the copyright owner. Requests for permission to make copies of any part of the work should be mailed to: Copyright Permissions, Steck-Vaughn Company, P.O. Box 26015, Austin, TX 78755.
Printed in the United States of America.
British edition Copyright © 1994 Evans Brothers.

1 2 3 4 5 6 7 8 9 00 PO 00 99 98 97 96 95 94

Watch Out for Strangers

Paul Humphrey and
Alex Ramsay

Illustrated by
Colin King

STECK-VAUGHN
COMPANY
ELEMENTARY · SECONDARY · ADULT · LIBRARY

"Hi, Mrs. Chang!"

"May we come and see your new kittens?"

"Yes, but you must ask your dad first."

Why do we have to ask Dad?

He will worry if he doesn't know where we are.

Always ask a parent if you want to go somewhere.

Dad, may we go with Mrs. Chang to see her new kittens?

Yes, but make sure you're home for supper at six o'clock.

Your mom or dad must know what time you are coming home.

Then they can look for you if you are late.

Aren't the kittens cute? Look at that little orange one.

That's my favorite! I wish we could keep it.

11

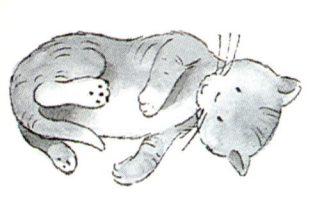

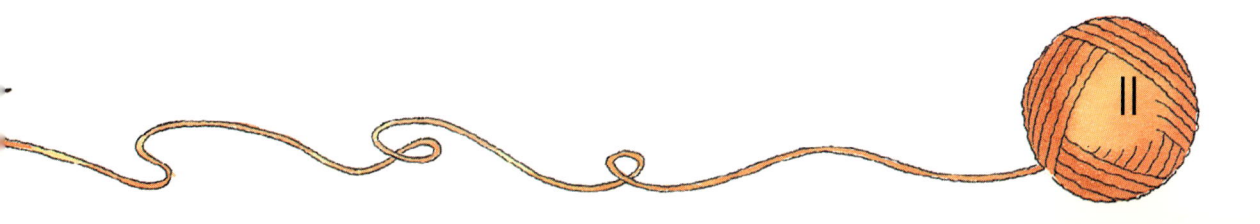

It's time for us to go home now.

I'll watch you from here to make sure you are safe.

14

"Do you want to stop at the park for a few minutes?"

"No! Remember that Dad says we must always walk straight home."

There are Dad's friends, Mr. and Mrs. Adams. They're in a new car.

Can we give you a ride somewhere?

No, thank you, Dad is waiting for us.

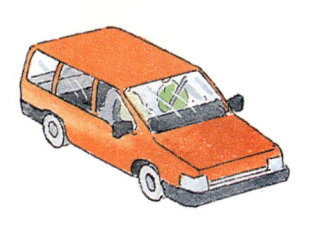

Never get in a car with
a stranger or even someone
you know. Always ask your
mom or dad first.

My teacher said that some people who look nice can hurt children.

Strangers might say Mom or Dad asked them to pick us up. But we should never go with them.

Remember, it's not rude to say no. Nice people will never mind your saying that.

Sometimes people offer
children nice things,
such as ice cream or
a trip to the zoo.

Never talk to strangers. Always say no if they offer you treats.

21

"If a stranger offered me sweets, I would say no.

You should always tell someone about it, too.

You can tell your teacher,
a parent, or a police officer.

Look, we're just in time for supper!

24

Mr. and Mrs. Adams offered us a ride in their new car. But we said no.

You did the right thing. Never go with anyone without asking me first.

"You have been very smart."

"I know. First we asked to go with Mrs. Chang.

Then we came straight home."

Mrs. Chang said we could have one of her kittens.

You have been very good today. We'll choose a kitten tomorrow!
Yippee!

Rules to Remember

1. Always be sure your mom or dad knows where you are (see pages 6-8).

2. Make sure your mom or dad knows what time you are coming home (see pages 8-9).

3. Never get in a car or go with someone without asking your mom or dad first (see pages 16-19).

4. Never talk to strangers or take treats from them (see pages 20-23).

5. Remember, it's always OK to say no! (see page 19)

32